Here they come – puffing and grunting,

towels flapping, caps flying.

"Wait for me!" calls Little Bob.

His small green hands grip his

swimming ring tightly.

The rains are over.

The waterhole is full…

Tales from the
WATERHOLE

Bob Graham

WALKER BOOKS

AND SUBSIDIARIES

LONDON · BOSTON · SYDNEY · AUCKLAND

Tales from the

FRUIT SALAD SWIMSUIT

FOOTBALL MATCH

DAREDEVIL STUNT

HOLIDAY

LONG RAINS PARTY

WATERHOLE

_____ page 6

_____ page 14

_____ page 30

_____ page 42

_____ page 52

For Oliver –
a smile that lights up the room

First published 2004 by Walker Books Ltd
87 Vauxhall Walk, London SE11 5HJ

2 4 6 8 10 9 7 5 3

© 2004 Bob Graham

The right of Bob Graham to be identified as author/illustrator
of this work has been asserted by him in accordance
with the Copyright, Designs and Patents Act 1988

This book has been typeset in Avenir Book

Printed in China

British Library Cataloguing in Publication Data:
a catalogue record for this book is
available from the British Library

ISBN 0-7445-6593-6

www.walkerbooks.co.uk

FRUIT SALAD
SWIMSUIT

It was a warm and lazy evening.

Morris watched TV with his best friend, Billy.

Mum read her Dry Season mail-order catalogue.

Dad snored.

"This is a lovely swimsuit. What do

you think, dear?" Mum asked Dad.

Dad raised an eyelid. "You look gorgeous in anything you wear," he said, and went back to sleep after a hard day lying in the sun. "Brrrrm," said Morris' little brother, Bob, under the table.

Two days later, Mum had her
new swimsuit.
"Well, what do you think, boys?
It's called 'Tropicana' in the catalogue,"
she said.

"You look lovely, Mum,"
Morris said loudly.
Billy leant towards Morris.
"Don't say it, Billy,"
said Morris, with his
mouth all thin.

But Billy whispered right into Morris' ear,

"Your mum looks like a fruit salad."

"You just wait, Billy," said Morris.

They went outside

and beat each

other up.

Well, they circled

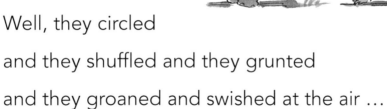

and they shuffled and they grunted

and they groaned and swished at the air …

9

until Billy finished on his shell,

so Morris had to help him up.

10

But, like all good friends,
they made up afterwards.
"Have you two been fighting?"
asked Morris' mum.
"Not really," said Billy.
"It was nothing," said Morris.
Little Bob made a scribble
with his finger in
the dust on
Billy's shell.

What colour and sparkle Morris' mum
brought to the waterhole!
Because they were friends, Billy said
nothing more about her looking
like a fruit salad.
And Morris said nothing about
Billy's mum looking a little like …
a rose garden.

FOOTBALL MATCH

orris' sneakers squeaked

on the bathroom floor.

Morris sniffed.

The room smelt of powder, perfume

and cod-flavoured toothpaste.

14

"Mum, I'm going to mess about down
at the waterhole," said Morris.
Mum dabbed at her lipstick.
"Well, I'm going out for the afternoon,"
she said, "so ask your father first."
She put a big wet kiss on his cheek.
"And take Little Bob with you," she added.

Morris went to find Dad.

Little Bob followed.

"Can I go to the waterhole?" Morris asked.

Dad stretched. Flies buzzed in the heat.

"You've got lipstick on your cheek,

Morris," he said.

"Oh," said Morris. He smeared

at the spot. "Can I?"

"If you take Little Bob," Dad said,

"and be home by sundown."

On the way to the waterhole

they met Billy.

"You brought a ball," said Billy.

"Yep," replied Morris.

He neatly swerved the ball

around Billy – who, being

a tortoise, was slow

on his feet.

"And you brought

Little Bob.

Hi, Bob,"

said Billy.

"Hello, Billy," said Little Bob, shyly.

   The remains of his lunch

   were all down his front.

   (Pilchard and chips.)

"Mucky, isn't he?" Billy said.

"Yeah, well … he's all right

   sometimes," said Morris.

"Let's go."

Morris and Billy's friends were
kicking an old tin can around.
"Here's Morris!" yelled Leon Lion.
"He's got a ball!" said Lucy Leopard.
"And a splodge on his cheek,"
grunted Harpo Hippo as
Morris arrived, puffing.

They picked teams.
(No one wanted Little Bob
or Slow Billy.)
But the two teams were soon
to become one, because …

22

over the hill came the mums!
They were returning very merry
from their afternoon together.
"FOOTBALL!" they yelled,
and tucked their skirts up high.

"Mums against the kids!"
said Morris' mum.
"Oh no," groaned Morris.

Mrs Elephant played in goal for the mums.

Billy played in goal for the kids

(with Little Bob on his back for extra height).

Mrs Elephant kicked off and returned to goal.

Mrs Hippo took the ball upfield

in a damaging run.

Morris' mum made a fine cross,

and Mrs Giraffe headed it in for a—

"GOAL!" yelled the mums.

How they celebrated!

25

That goal was the first of many.

Slow Billy and Little Bob tried their best,

but the mums won 17-0.

There was no contest. Not really.

But while the mums were giving

the whole team a present

of big red splodgy kisses

(just like Morris') ...

Little Bob managed to roll the ball
into the mums' goal with his little feet.
"Goal!" he squeaked.
"17-1!" yelled Morris.
And the kids celebrated too.

DAREDEVIL
STUNT

It was a hot and busy afternoon.

Roars, grunts, squeaks and squeals filled the air.

Morris was making some tricky moves on his

skateboard, mainly to impress Wendy Warthog,

who was ignoring him completely.

"Look at me, I'm a jumbo jet!"
called Tessa Elephant,
as she took off from
the springboard.

Tessa belly-flopped, and water
came down like a shower of rain.
"Tell you what I'll do," said Morris to Wendy,
"I'll do you a STUNT."

Gerard Giraffe and Leon Lion

glanced at Morris.

Harpo Hippo turned his head.

Zoe Zebra moved for a better look.

And Wendy still ignored Morris.

As the pool settled, Morris went up on the bank.

"Here's my daredevil trick!" he shouted.

"Harpo, Billy and Little Bob, you get in the water.

Harpo, hold the springboard down…

When I come racing down, Harpo, you let go.
I will go up in the air and over the three of you …
and land on the other side."

A muffled snort came
from under Wendy's book.

Billy and Little Bob floated and waited.

Harpo held the springboard.

All was silent round the waterhole.

"Here he comes," squealed

Little Bob from his rubber ring.

From under her book,

Wendy took a tiny peek.

Morris hit the board at speed ...

just as a tick bird landed on Harpo's nose.

"AAAAACHOOOO!"

"Too early, too early!"
yelled Morris, who was
himself too late to stop.
Out of control,
he somersaulted high in the air,

once –

twice –

and landed in the soft mud,

SQUELCH!

But he was quick to his feet
with a little skip and a jump.
Wendy put down her book.
"Not bad," she grunted.
"Needs a little more practice, though."
"It's the first time I have ever missed,"
 said Morris.
"But it's the first time you've
 ever tried," said Billy.
Morris gave him a withering look.

"My mum wants me home by sundown,"
said Wendy, gathering her things.
"We should all be off home, then,"
said Morris, walking tall –
Wendy had spoken to him.
Twice.

HOLIDAY

Waldo Wildebeest was not happy.

"We're going on a walking holiday tomorrow."

He waved a hoof in the direction of the horizon.

"Oh, not good!" replied Morris and Billy.

"We go every year," Waldo continued,

"with my zillions of relatives. We always

stop someplace boring to eat. And I have to

look after all the little kids."

"Like I do with Little Bob?" Morris asked.

"Like about a hundred Little Bobs," said Waldo.

"The absolute worst thing,"

he went on, "is crossing the rivers.

We get all our stuff wet,

and my sneakers get muddy.

And I HATE IT!"

Morris had an idea.

He went home and asked his dad.

"What? The dinghy?" said Morris' dad.

"No, Waldo's family can't borrow it.

I need it for my fishing."

"You never use it," said Mum.

She slapped her tail once on the floor.

So the dinghy went overland on

Dad's back to the Wildebeests' house.

"For the river crossings," Morris said.

"Wicked!" said Waldo.

Morris' mum prodded her husband in the back.

"Hmm … yes, well, just pull this cord and

she should start," said Dad.

"Let's have some tea," suggested Waldo's mum.

Morris' family sat down to tea and
rye-grass cakes with the Wildebeests.
There was a pause in the conversation.
"Any special plans for the holiday?"
Morris' dad asked.

Grandad Wildebeest replied,
"No, just eatin' … and walkin' …
and eatin' … and walkin'."
Waldo looked at Morris
and rolled his eyes.

The next morning, Morris, Billy and Little Bob
watched Waldo's big family trudge past.
Waldo waved from inside a crowd of small
wildebeest. His old pushchair carried the dinghy.
(It may carry him too, soon.)

"Would you feed our fish, Morris?"
called Waldo's mum.

"Just a pinch of food a day."

"Sure," replied Morris.

"See you, Waldo."

49

Later at Waldo's house, Billy,

Morris and Little Bob looked

at the tropical fish.

"Poor Waldo," said Billy.

"All those little kids to look after."

"Makes me feel lucky – nearly!" said Morris.

He patted his brother's bumpy head

almost fondly.

LONG RAINS
PARTY

ld trousers were quite OK

round the waterhole.

No trousers too.

Except for special occasions,

like the Long Rains Party.

"Look at you, Morris," said his mum.

"The Long Rains are coming and you have

nothing for the party. Those jeans

are so old you can see through them.

We'll have to go shopping."

Morris hunched in despair.

He hated shopping.

At the "Lazy Q Ranch", Morris saw Gerard Giraffe.
"I have to get new jeans for the party," Gerard
said miserably. The assistant came over.
"These are our new Range Riders,"
she said. "They may be a bit short
in the leg…"

"He's long in the leg," said Gerard's mum.

"Takes after his father."

Morris' legs, on the other hand,

were so short they could fit in

Gerard's pockets…

"Try these on, Morris,"
said his mum. "Never mind
the legs. It's the hole for the
tail that needs to be right."
Tall Gerard was well-covered
by the changing-room doors.
But not Morris
(being so short in the leg).
"Do we have to do this?"
he asked.
"Of course," replied his mum.
"The Warthogs will have
Wendy turned out pretty
as a picture."
"Oh…" said Morris.

"Hmm," said the mums.

They looked at each other.

"We can get the scissors out…"

said Morris' mum.

"And the sewing machine…"

said Gerard's mum

"Oh no!" groaned Morris and Gerard.

"We'll take them," said the mums.

It was of course an obvious

solution to the problem.

A snip here.

A stitch there.

The leg that came off

Morris' jeans ...

went onto Gerard's.

And the whole thing was a misery

throughout for the two friends.

At the party, Wendy Warthog did indeed look as beautiful as an oil painting. Billy's shell sparkled and Little Bob stayed clean for two whole minutes.

61

Billy's mum wanted a photo.

Gerard, Harpo, Tessa, Waldo, Zoe,
Lucy, Wendy, Leon, Morris, Billy
and Little Bob shuffled together.
"Where did you get those jeans, Morris?"
Wendy Warthog said out of the corner
of her mouth. "You look seriously cool!"
Morris blushed from his nose right
to the tip of his otherwise green tail.
"Er … right … thanks," he said.

"Smile, everyone!" Billy's mum called.

The camera clicked.

Some large black spots appeared in the dust.

The Long Rains had arrived.

A new season had begun.